MY MAGIC MIRROR

By: Anushka Bhattacharjee

To Coco and Lilou,

Enjoy the book!

Anushka

Prologue

"Do we have to move?" I ask for the hundredth time. "Yes, and no complaining," my mom says, annoyed. Hpmh. It's not she who has to leave her friends without any way to connect with them. My mom can just call her friends on her cell phone. But do I have a cell phone? No, I do not. Although I would totally love one. Anyways, how do I connect with my friends daily? We don't have a telephone so I'll only be able to call my friends, like once a week. I grumble some not-so-nice words under my breath as I get inside the car to go to Toronto, Canada.

CHAPTER 1

THE MAGIC MIRROR IN MY HOUSE

My life was all normal, but then things had to change.

My name is Ara. I'm 9 and I have a brother named Felice who is 5 years old.

Also, I am new to Toronto and things are just so different here. All I want to do is go back to Arizona, but that's just me.

My brother is not too sad, he doesn't miss his friends too much because he already got a new friend, Aziz.

But I haven't made any new friends here because of all the weird things.

Sometimes I ask my mom, why we had to move and my mom always says, "Because I've got a really good business job," and she ends the conversation.

✳ ✳ ✳ ✳ ✳ ✳ ✳ ✳ ✳ ✳ ✳ ✳ ✳ ✳ ✳ ✳ ✳ ✳

One day, I was dreaming about going back to Arizona when my brother (rudely) shook me awake.

"Ara! the mirror in the basement is shaking!" yelled my brother.

"Felice, that doesn't make sense," I say.

"Look for yourself," says my brother.

I go have a look because I do not want Felice to annoy me for the rest of the night. I go down to the basement and I'm shocked to see...

The mirror is SHAKING!!!!

I get closer to inspect and accidentally bump into it. It glows yellow and then it starts to suck us in.

"Ahhh!!!!" I scream.

Meanwhile my brother looks like he's having fun.

Can you believe that? My brother could have fun if a 10 feet alligator was looking for a very certain meal-us!

I look around, hoping to find something to hold on to, but our basement is empty except for some old boxes that could never support our weight.

We go falling into the mirror.

* * * * * * * * * * * * * * * * * * *

(Note: make sure when/if we get home, put some heavy things in the basement, in case this happens again)

The first thing I see is a house.

Beside it I see three pigs bid goodbye to another pig that looks like their mom.

The weird thing is that, the pigs are standing on their back legs, like people. "Be safe, and look out for the big, bad wolf," the mom pig said.

The big, bad wolf. Three pigs. A mommy pig saying "bye". Four pigs standing on their back legs.

Something weird is happening in my head.
It's like I know these people but I don't. Which doesn't make sense.

It's kind of like those questions where they ask,
"If plural goose is geese and plural mouse is mice why isn't plural moose meese?"
OR
"Which came first, the chicken or the egg?"

"AHHHHHHHHHHH! Ara we're not in Toronto!" Felice screams.

"I know that Felice," I say. Those pigs look oddly familiar but I've never seen them.

For the first time ever, I want to go back to Toronto.

While we're talking, the 'baby' pigs leave, so we go up to the house.

The mommy pig greets us and says, "You children should come inside," and she takes us inside the house.

"My poor pigs! I gave them some money to buy materials to make houses," she says, a bit to herself and a bit to us, as she takes us to the living room.

Suddenly I know where we are.

"Felice, we have to go!" I tell Felice.

"Thank you, Mrs. Pig but we have somewhere to go," I say.

"Ok," shrugs the pig.

Once we're out of the house I shout again "Felice, I know where we are!"

* * * * * * * * * * * * * * * * * *

"We're in the story of the three little pigs," I shout. I can't help myself.

"We can't be!" my brother is looking at me like I'm crazy.

"We are and I have proof," I say.

"There is a big, bad wolf, three little pigs that talk and walk on their hind legs and a mommy pig saying bye to them. Isn't that enough proof?"

"I guess so, but how did we get here?" my brother says, a bit hesitant.

"I don't really know but I think it's magic," I say.

"Do you remember how our mirror shook and glowed yellow. Normal mirrors don't do that, and don't you have this creepy feeling that something is inside the mirror?"

"At least we know where we are though; that's good."

Chapter2

The story of The Three Little Pigs

"I think we should go over what happens in the story," I say.

"Um, Ara I don't really know how the story goes," my brother whispers. I roll my eyes. I'm not surprised that my brother doesn't know how the story goes because he is always watching T.V.

Me? I'll admit, I watch TV a lot but I also read books, and a few days ago I read ***The Three Little Pigs*** book.

"Ok, I'll tell you, so get comfy,'' I grumble.

"Once there was a mommy pig and three little pigs. When they got old enough, the 'little pigs' (I make air quotes) went out of their house to seek their destiny. Their mom said, "beware of the big bad wolf." The first and second pig weren't so smart. The first pig built his house out of straw and when the wolf came, he said "little pig come outside" and the pig said "not by the hairs of my chinny chin chin." So, the wolf huffed and puffed and he blew the straw house down. Then he gobbled up the pig. The second pig was about one and a half times as smart. He made his house out of sticks and the same thing that happened to the first pig happened to him. The third pig was about 1 million times as smart as his brothers. He made his house out of bricks and when the wolf came, he said the same thing he said to the other pigs. When the pig said 'no', the wolf tried to blow the house down but he couldn't. Over the next few days, the wolf tried to get the pig outside and the pig knew that he would keep coming back. The next time the wolf came he asked if the pig wanted to go with him to the farmer's market. The pig said yes and they planned to meet at 5 o'clock. The next day at 4 o'clock the pig went out of the house and got apples from the farmer's market. When the wolf came at 5 o'clock the pig said that he already went to the farmer's market. The wolf got angry, so he climbed up the house and went down the chimney. The pig knew what the wolf was going to do for some reason and he put a boiling pot of water under the chimney. When the wolf came down the chimney he got boiled and the pig ate him ---The End!" I finish.

My voice is a bit raspy. "That story is cool," my brother says.

"Felice we should find a way to get home," I say. "Let's explore a bit and with luck we will find a way to get back home."

"OK!" my brother says, and off we go.

✶ ✶ ✶ ✶ ✶ ✶ ✶ ✶ ✶ ✶ ✶ ✶ ✶ ✶ ✶ ✶ ✶ ✶

We have been walking for a while when I feel a bit queasy. You see, our parents don't know where we are, and they could be calling the police by now.

My watch is on my wrist and I see it is 1:00. Strange, we've been here for about 2 hours. So, every hour there, is 2 hours here. My parents wake up at 7:00, so we have 12 hours to find a way to get home. Weird, but good.

"Felice," I say, "We have 12 hours here to get back to our house."

"Good!" says my brother.

We walk a little farther and my brother asks, "Ara, what if we saved the pigs? I mean, what if we stop the wolf from eating the first two pigs, and maybe, instead of the wolf being eaten by the third pig, why don't we just let the police handle that."

"Good idea," I say. I can't believe my brother thought of that plan before me. "But first we have to find out where the first pig is."

"That shouldn't be hard," my brother says. "We just find a pig and ask what material his house is made out of."

Soon we reached the town, and what I see, makes my jaw drop to the ground. There are pigs everywhere and they are just like humans, except they're pigs.

"Right, that complicates things a bit," my brother says nervously. "Ara, what should we do now?"

 "I think we should ask a pig what town this is," I reply. We walk to a cheese store. Who knew pigs ate cheese? I sure didn't.

"Mrs. Pig do you know what the name of this town is?" I say to a pig in the store.

"You should know the town's name is Pown," the pig replies, annoyed. "Pown means pig town," she explains grumpily when she sees our confused faces.

I say "thank you" and leave.

Pigs are giving us funny looks and I suddenly realize that there are no humans.

I tell Felice that we should find some pig costumes and we go back to the meadow.

Soon we reach an abandoned house and inside it we see pig costumes and some pig masks and we put on two. Hopefully the owner won't notice that we took some of his or her costumes.

When we leave, I can't help but wonder why the costumes were there.

So far we haven't seen any living things except pigs. Hmm, I'll need to keep my eyes open to look for living things that aren't pigs.

＊＊＊＊＊＊＊＊＊＊＊＊＊＊＊＊＊

We walk back to Pown with our pig costumes.
I sneak a peek at my watch. It says that it's 1:10 on my watch so we've been walking 20 minutes.

I don't know about you but I am not very athletic. I'm not so great in gym class. It's the only class, other than writing, where I get B's.

When we get back to town, we see that all the pigs are talking about us. I look at Felice and Felice looks at me nervously.

Thankfully, just in front of us we see a black, medium-sized pig giving some money to another pig in exchange for a pile of straw.

We both see him walk out into the meadow again and we follow him. I'm walking a lot today.

When the first pig is in the countryside I ask, "Excuse me, but what is your name?"

"Tom," the pig replies.

Hmm, I wonder what his house is made out of. But I can't just ask him that. It would be too weird.

Luckily the pig said "I'm about to make my house."

My heart skips a beat. "Really?" I ask. "What is it made of?"

"Straw," Tom answers.

Yay! I could cry! This has to be the first pig!!!!

"Listen," I tell Tom, "You have to change the material you are using for your house."

Tom looks, understandably, confused. "Why?" he asks.

Oh no, if we talk about the big, bad wolf he will ask how we know, and that will be way too weird.

As I am thinking about what to do, my brother says, "Because strong winds might destroy your house."

Chapter 3
Tom's evil brother

"Hmm," says Tom, "You may be right." But then he looks worried.

"What will we do?" he asks.

"We can make it out of wood," I say, but Tom just shakes his head.

"I don't have enough money. My evil older brother stole half of my money so he could have a better house. That's why I have to make my house out of straw. It is the only building material I can afford," he says.

That's so sad.

"Do you pigs have any money? And by the way, what are your names?" he asks.

Pigs? Oh, right. Because of our pig costumes he thinks that Felice and I are pigs. Wow!

These pig costumes work really well. I'm starting to think that they're disguises because no way a costume creator would try and make these so realistic.

"Wait a minute," I say "Can you keep a secret?"

"Yeah," Tom answers.

Me and Felice tell Tom everything except for the part that we came here via a mirror, and that we know how his and his brothers' story goes.

We told him that we were just visiting Pown.

Speaking of Tom's brothers, I wonder who the evil one is. Is it the second pig or the third pig?

How can I ask him that? Wait. I know! "Do you know what your brother's house is made out of?" I ask Tom.

"Which one? I have 2," Tom says

"The evil one," I reply.

"Bricks, I think," Tom answers.

The evil brother has to be the third pig.

Meanwhile, Felice is playing with some pigs about his age. I think that will keep him from getting into trouble, so me and Tom can continue chatting.

Tom tells me that his evil brother's name is Titan, and his nice brother's name is Owen. He also tells me that he thinks he knows the hotel Titan is in and how to get there!

Yay! So, all we have to do is break into Titan's house and get the money he stole from Tom!

At first Tom is a bit hesitant because he doesn't want to steal but when I tell him that we aren't exactly stealing, most of his hesitation goes away.

"Let's tell Felice," I say to Tom. So, we do.

"Awesome!" my brother shouts when he hears the plan. Although it might be because we are breaking into a hotel.

So, after we have lunch, we start walking to Titan's hotel. If this was walk-a-thon I would win it.

We walk to the hotel. Felice is lagging behind because he's sad to say goodbye to his friends, but we have a plan.

First, we help Tom get his money back.

Next, we help Owen from getting eaten by the Big Bad Wolf.

Then we get the Big Bad Wolf arrested.

Finally, we find a way to get home.

It's a great plan, isn't it? I should be a planner when I'm older. Although I don't know if that's a real job. Maybe I'll just be a doctor. Or a firefighter. Or a judge. Or an astronomer. Or an engineer. I don't know. The possibilities are endless. Maybe I'll just stick to being a kid for now.

Anyway, when we get to the lobby, we ask that person that's always on the other side of the desk in hotels, which room Titan is in. Tom also says his last name just in case there are two Titan's, which I'm pretty sure there aren't.

"Room 111," the person behind the desk says when we tell her that we're visiting Titan.

We walk until we reach room 111.

Titan is very irresponsible; he has left his door open. Who knows, a mad man can break into his room whenever he wants to. But that's good for us.

"Thank Goodness!" Tom says, "Titan never closes doors. Except when he's in the bathroom."

"Let's get the money quick," I tell Felice and Tom, "Titan could get inside any minute."

"Right. Captain Ara!" Felice jokes, saluting me, but I shush him. This is not the time for telling jokes.

"How much did Titan steal from you?" I ask Tom.

"He stole $25 from me so I only had $25 left and straw was the only material I could buy for a house with $25."

I quickly look around for 25 dollars. It isn't hard. I spot a $20 note and a $5 note on the bedside table.

Then suddenly I hear footsteps coming. Tom, Felice, and I freeze in our tracks.

But luckily, it's just a worker coming down the hall to help some very picky customers. We hightail it out of the hotel.

Just as we're running through the lobby, we hear an ear-piercing scream.

"Someone stole my money!" Titan screams.

Uh-oh. Me, Tom, and Felice, go, go, go!

* * * * * * * * * * * * * * * * *

After we're about a half a mile away from the hotel we stop to take a breath.

"That... puff...was...puff...close!" my brother says.

"Way too close for my liking," I say.

"But the good thing is that we have the money, so I can buy a wooden house that has at least 4 rooms including a kitchen and a bathroom," Tom says.

Things in Pown sure are cheap. I mean, only $50 for a wooden house. Although it's probably small.

I was wrong. When we walk to the place where Tom's going to buy his house, I'm shocked. All the houses on this street are the size of my house and my house definitely wasn't worth $50.

We keep walking down the street until we reach a house that has a sign that says, **"FOR SALE"**. What luck! "This house is perfect!" I say after we finish touring the house.

Tom thinks so too, so he calls the owners.

"Hello this is Tom Willow speaking." (Willow is Tom's last name). "Yes, I happened to come across your house and I would like to buy it. WHAT! It's only $40!"

Then Tom starts saying things like "Awesome! Great. Thanks! Goodbye!"

After the call ends, he looks at us. His face is shining.

"The owners are really nice," he tells me and Felice, "and the cost is only $40 so I can use the rest for my job. I want to be a doctor."

"Great! But first you have to return the straw," I say.

The first part of the mission is success!

Then I say to Tom "It was really nice to meet you but we need to get going."

"OK," Tom says.

He seems sad but he understands. Also, his new house should cheer him up.

So, Felice and I go back to the cheese shop, and hopefully we'll find the second pig there, or somewhere close by.

Chapter 4: Owen

We start walking towards the cheese shop.

Soon Felice and I take a break near a stream. Felice plays in the water with some fish, while I go and rest under a tree.

I look up. Felice has been strangely quiet for the past 10 minutes. I look at the stream. Felice isn't there.

"Felice, come!" I demand. No answer. "Felice come now," I say, starting to get worried.

"BOO!" Felice shouts jumping out from a tree I didn't notice before. He splashed some water on me. I don't know how to react.

Then, a sneaky plan comes to my mind.

"Ahhhhh! You've sprayed water on my watch and it isn't waterproof," I fake-cry. It actually is waterproof but I don't think Felice remembers that.

Felice gasps, "Oh no. Do you remember what time it was?" He asks.

When I say no Felice asks if he can see the watch. "Ok," I tell him. But first I switched the button.

Now it's showing the local time instead of time back home. It shows 2:00 and that's obviously not the time at our house.

Felice starts crying like a baby so I shout "Pranked you!" and I explain the whole trick.

Luckily Felice gets over it quickly. He just keeps saying that when he has a watch, he's going to try that on me.

We walk the rest of the way.

* * * * * * * * * * * * * * * * *

Wow. Luck is definitely on our side today.

At the cheese shop we see a short pig with a hat about to give three $10 bills to another pig in exchange for a humongous pile of sticks. Where is the other $20 dollars? Maybe this is the wrong pig. I'll ask him if his name is Owen.

"Excuse me," I ask "What is your name?"

"Owen," the pig answers. Great!

This is the second pig!

Meanwhile, the stick seller is muttering some not-so-nice words and she's leaving.

"Wait!" Owen says, but I stop him.

"It's ok," I tell him. "You don't need her anyway."

"I do, sticks are the only good material I can buy with $30. I used to have $50 and that was enough to buy a house made of logs, but I don't know where the other $20 is," Owen says, struggling to get out of my grasp.

But I'm strong, so he can't get away.

"Listen," I say, and Owen stops struggling.

"You need to find your $20 bill because sticks aren't strong. Me and Felice will help you find it, won't we Felice?" I finish.

"Right!" Felice says. I love how he always has my back.

"I might have forgotten it. I'm very forgetful sometimes," Owen admits. "Oh, and by the way, my name's Owen," he introduces himself.

Me and Felice introduce ourselves too. "My name is Ara and this is Felice," I tell Owen.

Then I ask, just like a detective "Owen, when did you figure out that it was missing?"

"An hour ago," Owen says, "But I had it in the morning when I went out of my house so it has gone missing this afternoon."

"What did you do this afternoon?" I ask Owen.

"Well, first I came here to buy some wood so I could build a house because I like building. Next, I went to a meadow for a picnic. Then I put something under my hat. And after that I found some wood that I liked but that's when I found out that my money was stolen," he recounts.

"What did you put under your hat?" I ask, curious to know. "I don't remember," Owen says.

Oh well, it was probably some rocks he liked. If I had the time, I would definitely collect some rocks. They're so pretty in Pown.

"Anyhow, let's start looking all over here," Felice says.

"Actually, I have already looked here, so we don't need to go again," Owen tells us.

"Then let's go to the meadow," Felice says, and he runs ahead of us. I shake my head. My brother is so impatient.

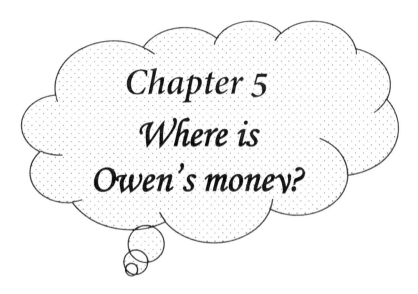

Chapter 5
Where is Owen's money?

Owen and I hurry and we catch up with Felice.

"What took you so long slow pokes?" my brother teases.
I stick my tongue out at him.

Then Owen starts leading the way.

As we're walking, I look at my watch. It says it's 2:00 at home, so we still have 10 hours. That's plenty of time. I hope.

When we finally reach the meadow, I say to Owen and Felice "I think we should take a break from walking."

"Yeah, my feet are tired," Felice complains.

So, we take a break and while Felice climbs some trees, me and Owen talk.

I tell him the exact same thing that I told Tom, you know, about us being not real pigs and that we're visiting Pown.

I know what you're thinking, I know, it's bad to lie but it's just too strange to say "Hi there! I just got slurped up by my magic mirror" or "Hi, I got here via mirror." See my point now? I thought you would. I'm very good at making others see my point.

Then we play hide-and-seek. Felice wins. He chooses the extreme hiding places. He climbed on top of a tree to hide there!

When my legs finally feel like legs again, we start looking around. Or at least, me and Owen. Felice is doing more playing than looking.

I shake my head. Little brothers! "Felice, look, instead of playing!" I command.

"Ok Ara," Felice grumbles "I was just having a little bit of fun."

"We have a mission," I say.

"Well, why can't we have fun while we're doing the mission?" Felice asks.

"Because…because…Ugh, you're impossible!" I snap.

Luckily Owen breaks up the fight before it gets too big.

"Felice, you already played so you have to do what your sister says," he tells Felice. "But Ara, Felice is right too. You guys can have fun while looking for the money,'' he says to me.

Hmph. I guess he's right. Also, I want to have a bit of fun. We spend 2 hours, which is 1 hour back home, trying to find Owen's $20 bill, but as they say, luck always runs out. Why did it have to run out now? Now, of all times.

We continue searching for another 15 minutes in vain.

By now we must've searched the entire meadow. "I don't think it's here," Owen says sadly, "And nobody could have taken it because no one comes here. It must have been carried away by the wind."

"But it wasn't windy today," I tell them. "Let's make a list about what could have happened to it."
We start making a list. It goes like this:

❌1.Somebody stole it-No, because no one comes here.

❌2.The wind carried it away-No, because it wasn't windy.

❌3.It fell in the lake-No, because it needed wind to do that and there's no wind.

✳ ✳ ✳ ✳ ✳ ✳ ✳ ✳ ✳ ✳ ✳ ✳ ✳ ✳ ✳ ✳ ✳ ✳

"Ugh, this is useless," I complain.

"Too bad," Owen sighs. "I guess I do have to make a house out of sticks."

* * * * * * * * * * * * * * * * * *

We start walking back.

Part 2 of the mission is a failure.

I look at my watch. It says it's 3:30 so we have 7 hours left in Pown.

Even if we stop the wolf, strong winds could/would blow the house down.

* * * * * * * * * * * * * * * * * *

As we're walking, I find myself thinking about what Owen said when we first met him. He said that he was forgetful… and what was next, again? Oh, right he said he put something under his hat.

Wait! Owen put something under his hat. What if that 'thing' was his money!

"Owen, can you take off your hat?" I ask him.

It's a weird question but trust me, I know what I'm doing.

"Why?" he replies, startled by the odd question.

"You'll see." I say.

Owen's still confused, but curiosity got the better of him and so he shrugs, takes off his hat and just as I suspected, there's a $20 note.

Everyone is breathless. Then…

"THIS IS AWESOME!!" Owen shouts.

Me and Owen start celebrating. Felice would join but he's too busy grumbling to himself because he searched for 2 hours (One hour at home) to find the money but it was with him all along!

The celebrations last for a full 15 minutes when I remember that only half of our mission is complete.

We still need to get the wolf arrested and find a way home. Something tells me the last one will be harder than arresting the wolf.

"We have to go," I tell Owen.

He gives me the same, sad smile Tom gave me, says goodbye, and walks out of sight.

While Owen goes back to the main street, to buy some wood we walk in the opposite direction.

Hopefully luck is on our side again.

We walk into the forest. I know you're not supposed to go to places, especially forests without asking your parents, but mine are currently unreachable.

We walk a bit more. I feel like Hansel and Gretel, except there's no witch here. What if there is? No. This forest can't have a witch.

I look around uneasily.

Then I hear a crunch behind me. I jump. Oh. It's just my brother. "Scaredy cat. Scaredy cat! Ara is a scaredy cat!" Felice teases.

We walk deeper into the forest. I try to block out Felice's scaredy cat song.

"Ara is a scaredy cat, scaredy cat, scaredy cat. Ara is a scaredy cat, a scaredy, scaredy, scaredy cat." He is really getting on my nerves.

I hear a crunch ahead of me. Crunch. Crunch. Crunch. I look at Felice.

"Any chance that's you?" I whisper. "I thought that was you," Felice whisper-shouts back. Oh no.

The crunches are way too loud for an animal. Oh, please let it be a hiker and not the big bad wolf. We tip-toe to where the crunching sound is coming from. I see....

Chapter 6
The big, Not-so-bad, wolf

The wolf and a pig!

The pig is stomping, so that's where the crunching noise is coming from.

"Those brats, they stopped you from eating those pigs. They're mean too, so you should eat them as well."

"Umm, ok Titan," the wolf says.

Titan? As in Owen and Tom's brother? I don't believe it. I don't want to believe it. And who are the brats?

"They stole my money today," Titan says.

Oh. Me and Felice are the brats. Felice and I creep up from the bushes to get a better look at them.

The wolf is grey, standing just like pigs, and wearing clothes. Also, he's skinny. He must not eat too many pigs. I wonder why.

Titan looks a lot like his brothers except he's wearing a green shirt and blue pants.

"Are you sure they're bad guys? I would never forgive myself if I ate a good pig. Also, they need a lot of salt," the wolf says.

"Of course, I'm sure, you big fool!" Titan cries.

He sure is mean. Titan, not the wolf. And the wolf is not too bad. But that does not mean he is nice.

"I want you to track down those kids first. They might have already helped Owen be safe, and as for Tom, they already have," Titan says angrily.

He's definitely talking about us.

"So go get those brats and eat them. One is a girl and one's a boy. Then see if Owen is safe. If he isn't, blow his house down and eat him," He commands the wolf.

Yikes! Also, could he stop calling us brats?

"I'm off, so make sure that those brats and Owen are eaten. Also, there's another mean guy, his name is Mike and he lives here. If he doesn't come out even after all your tricks are finished try going down his chimney. Then eat him too," Titan points to a map.

Wait. That looks a lot like the third little pig's house in the book.

Of course! Why didn't I think of that! The map goes to Titan's house.

And that explains why Titan was in a hotel. He didn't want the wolf to know he had a house or the wolf would piece together the plan. Titan will pretend to be Mike.

I'll bet anything that Titan has a boiling pot of water at the bottom of the chimney and when the wolf goes down the chimney, he'll get boiled. Then Titan will eat him.

I bet this Mike guy doesn't even exist.

Hah! You're not as smart as you think Titan!

But do pigs really eat wolves? I thought it was the other way around. Oh well, I guess I was wrong.

I whisper Titan's 'master' plan to Felice.

His eyes are popping out of his head. Well, not really. But you get the idea.

Meanwhile, Titan leaves. Thankfully, he didn't spot us. When he's out of sight, the wolf does something shocking.

He cries! We cautiously walk to the wolf.

"Hi...sniff...there," The wolf says between sobs.

"Umm hi," I say, "Don't freak out or anything, but we're the kids Titan was talking about."

And then the wolf does exactly what I told him not to. "Ahhhhhhhh! PleaseDon'tDoAnythingToMe!" the wolf screams. I cover his mouth.

Do we want Titan to find out that the people he wants are right here? No, we do not.

I know what you're thinking. Ara, why did you tell the wolf? It's because I kind of trust him now that I've figured out the whole scheme.

Also, I haven't even *read* about bad guys who cry, much less see one.

When I finally convince the wolf that we're not bad guys, he stops screaming. Good. I was getting a headache.

"What's your name?" Felice asks the wolf.

"Bok," the wolf answers.

"Well, Bok," I say, "You've got the whole story tangled up," and Felice tells Titan's whole plan.

"So let me get this straight. Titan is making me kill his own brothers and two kids," Bok says.

"Yup," Felice replies.

"Making you?" I ask.

"Yeah. The wolf's and the pigs have a truce. Wolfs won't hunt pigs if pigs help defend us from humans who want to hunt us. I guess Titan is angry at his brothers or something," Bok says.

"That pig should be arrested," Felice shouts angrily. I can't help but agree.

It's definitely against the law to try to kill people…er, pigs. We keep peppering Bok with questions.

It seems that Titan asked Bok for some 'help' and Bok agreed because he's nice and you know the rest.

"Did Titan tell you where he was going?" I ask Bok.

"No, but he's usually at the costume shop at this time of the day."

"Ok then we're off to the costume shop." I say to everyone. Then I ask "Wait, where's the costume shop?"

"It's beside the cheese shop, I think," Bok tells us.

"I know where the cheese shop is, and how to get there so follow me!" I tell them.

"Can we play here a bit? Please," my brother pleads.

"Okay, okay," I say "Let's play tag on our way to the costume shop. You're it!" I tag Felice. "Hey! Not fair!" Felice shouts but he tries to catch me. He looks at Bok and Bok tries to run, but he's too late. Felice tags him.

Unfortunately, Bok's a lot faster than Felice and it's not Felice he's interested in. He runs towards me. I try to run away but Bok easily tags me.

"First one who gets tagged twice is the loser and the last one who gets tagged twice is the winner," Felice calls.

He doesn't notice where he's going. He's within arm's reach of me so I tag him.

Hah! He's the loser. Felice quickly tags me while I'm doing my victory dance so I'm second.

Bok (Unsurprisingly) is first.

"Enough playtime. Let's go get Titan," Bok says, clapping his hands.

"You're right. Felice, come on!" I say. We start walking back to the cheese shop.

I wish I could just press something and then I'd be instantly transported to the cheese shop. I look at my watch. It says 4:00 so we still have 6 hours left. That's great!

Chapter 7

Distracting Titan

When we finally reach the costume shop, we go to the manager.

"Um, excuse me, but do you know a certain pig named Titan?" I ask.

"Yes. He was here not so long ago. He's very interested in my pig costumes and masks," the manager replies.

I wonder why? He's a pig. So why does he need pig costumes? What if he's actually a squirrel?

No, that's silly. If Titan was a squirrel, then Owen and Tom would be squirrels and they're too nice to be pretending.

Maybe it's for Bok. Yeah! Bok probably has a lot of pig costumes so he can wander around and not draw attention to himself.

I turn to ask Bok but he looks like he's thinking about something.

He's _pondering_. That means he's thinking really hard. I have a high vocabulary. Last week I got a 10/10 on my spelling test and the words were really hard. I'm not kidding. They were all names of countries, towns, and cities. And those always have silent letters. Also, you have to put capitals on the first letter.

I decide to let him think and I turn to the manager.

"Do you know where he went?" I ask the manager.

"Nope," the manager says. Darn. We're back to square 1.

Meanwhile, Felice looks like he's figured something out.

"Okay, bye!" he says to the manager.

Then he pulls me out of the store. Bok follows.

"I know where Titan is!" he says.

"Remember the abandoned house where we got our pig costumes, Ara. We thought it was abandoned but it was actually Titan's house!"

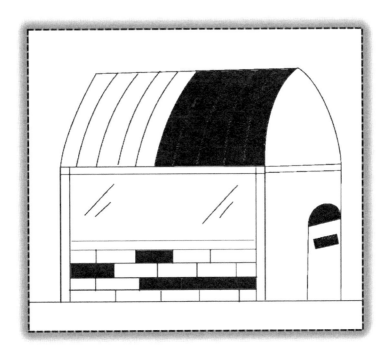

I shush him but it's too late. "You guys aren't pigs!" Bok says. "No, we're not," I admit. "We're humans and we're visiting Pown. But don't freak out or anything."

"AHHHHHHH! Humans are evil!" Bok screams.

"Umm, I don't mean to be rude but that's kind of dumb," Felice says.

"Is every wolf nice? Just because some wolves are not-so-nice does that mean that they are all not nice?"

"Well, I suppose you have a point," Bok says.

"So, what are we waiting for? Let's GO!" Felice says. I grab him by the sleeve. "Wait mister. I don't know where the house is."

"Then you're lucky I do," Felice gleefully shouts.

"You remember where it is?" I ask in complete shock.

"Yup!" Felice says, smirking. "It's behind the candy shop."

Now I get why he remembers where it is. Felice is in love with candy.

So, we follow Felice. We walk until we reach the candy shop. Then Felice stops.

"I don't know where to go after here," he admits sheepishly.

"I thought you knew where it is."

"Not really, I just said that I know how to get here," my brother mutters.

Then I look around. Wait! This place is familiar!

"I know how to get to Titan's hiding place!" I announce.

"Seriously? You're not leading us on a wild goose chase, are you?" Bok asks. Apparently, he's pretty ticked off because of Felice. I don't blame him.

"Nope." I tell him.

And after a thousand minutes, more or less a *lot* hundred we finally reach the 'abandoned' house.

We hear Titan saying to himself, "Now after that wolf goes to my house and when he tries all his tricks but they won't work, he'll try coming down the chimney and he'll get boiled! Hahahahaha!" He cackles.

Oh no. I have a big dilemma.

- ❖ If we all go to get the police then Titan could leave without us knowing.
- ❖ If we all stay here then the police won't know anything.

Me and Felice don't have a cell phone or any type of phone but I don't know about Bok.

"Bok," I whisper urgently. "Do you have a cell phone?"

"A cell-what?" He asks. I guess they don't have cell phones here.

Another reason I should have a cell phone.

What? You never know when your mirror might slurp you up and you end up needing a cell phone to catch a law-breaker.

So that leaves……ugh………splitting up.

I know what you're saying. Ara what's wrong with splitting up?

It's just that I don't want to risk losing my brother in this crazy place.

But we have to do what we have to do.

"We have to split up," I say.

"Felice and I will make sure that Titan doesn't get away. Bok, go get the police. Get them quick because I don't know how long he's going to stay here."

"Okay, I'll go to the cheese shop. It's near the police station." Bok says, and he leaves.

Is everything near the cheese shop? Anyway, I really hope he goes quick. I do not want to be stuck here with an angry pig. Especially a pig who wants to kill his own brothers.

We look through the windows to see what Titan is doing. Neither of us can look up so high so I give Felice a piggyback ride.

"I still can't see Ara," Felice smirks. I don't lift him higher because I know what he wants. He doesn't want to really see Titan; he just wants to be higher.

Also, I'm already having trouble holding up his weight now so I can't imagine what it would be if he went on my shoulders.

Felice, seeing that I won't budge, tries to climb onto my shoulders. I barely manage to stop him from toppling over and getting off me.

I'm debating whether I should take him down or keep him up. Most of the facts round to getting him down.

While I'm debating Felice climbs to my shoulders again.

"Yay! I got to your shoulders!" Felice cheers.

I can't help it. My knees start to buckle and we fall to the ground.

Ouch. Thankfully Felice did not fall on me.

"Oops!" Felice mumbles. "I'm sorry Ara."

Well, that won't do any good now. Then I hear it. Thump. Thump. Thump.

"Who's there? Who made that noise?" Titan screeches. Uh-oh.

"Forget about that. Hide!" I hiss to my brother.

I hide in some bushes, while Felice climbs up a tree. I hope that Titan doesn't see my hair. I quickly flatten it. But not quick enough.

"Hey! You! Were you spying on me?" asks Titan.

"No," I lie, but he knows that I'm lying.

Titan looks so angry I think he might explode! I brace myself, but before Titan can even touch me, an acorn hits him in the head. Huh?

"What is going o-ouch!" he cries as another acorn hits him on the head. We look up and we see Felice to the rescue!

"Run, Ara, run," Felice shouts to me as he keeps bonking acorns on Titan's head.

I don't need to be told twice, I run for it. When I'm a good distance away I look back. Felice had a pile of acorns but there are hardly any of them left. When the acorns run out Felice quietly slips away.

Titan is still rubbing his head from the acorn and Felice catches up to me.

I'm happy that he got away but I'm mad that he tried to climb on me.

"Why did you climb on me?" I grumble-ask.

"Well," Felice turns bright red. "It's ok. It worked out at the end."

"I nearly got caught, and you call that *ok!*?"

"But it's ok."

"Fine then. Let's look at all the things that are ok." I say sarcastically.

"One, my shoulders feel like they're about to break. Two, I have at least 10 bruises. Three, I almost got caught by Titan. And we're lucky he didn't recognize us or he would have killed us.''

Then Felice says "Sorry Ara."

"Whatever," I say. I'm still mad.

Then we hear a rumbling noise. Rumble. Rumble. Rumble.

Chapter 8
The capture of Titan

We see some cars. They all have police signs on them. They're here! Bok got the police after all!

"Officer Luna here. What's your name?" an officer asks me.

"My name's Ara and this is Felice," I stammer. I would be nervous talking to a cop at home and this is no exception.

Titan finally looks up and when he sees us, he starts running. He runs into a forest and we chase after him. It's foggy out here so I can't see. At all.

Then somebody grabs me by the hand. I scream. So does Felice.

"Ahhhhh!" we both scream.

I know that the hand is not Bok's because I feel hooves not paws.

I try to hold on to Felice, but have I mentioned before that it's very foggy and my hooves keep slipping from how damp it is. I have no idea how pigs do it. They probably know how to when they're born.

Anyway, I try to fight back to the pig who's holding me when I think that it could be a police officer.

And maybe he can't speak. That would explain why he's not talking to us.

That sort of thing happens in movies. The hero is captured by some monster and then he finds out it's a friend.

I stop struggling and let him/her drag me. Maybe he/she is trying to get us away from Titan. I motion to Felice to stop fighting. He does, thankfully. Whoever it is, let's go of me and Felice and we walk silently.

The fog finally clears up and I see that we're at the edge of the forest because of how thin the trees are.

See? I knew that the pig was good. I can definitely see that this is a boy but I don't know anything else because there is a mask covering his face and a too-big hat on his head.

When we get to the car, my blood freezes. There is no police sign on it.

Oh no, Oh no, Oh no, Oh no, Oh no.

This is Titan's car. Felice on the other hand doesn't realize it's not a police car, (who can blame him? He's only 5) and starts running towards it.

I grab him and I run at the speed of light. Well not really, but you get the idea.

Titan looks up but since he has the hat on, he has to take it off to see, and by the time he does, he's barely able to see us.

But barely isn't enough. He starts running to us. We run but he quickly catches up.

He's 50 yards away. 40 yards. 30 yards. When he's 25 yards away Felice says "Ara we need to climb this tree."

"What? But I don't know how," I protest.

"Well then, it's time to learn."

Humph. I'm supposed to be telling *him* what to do, not the other way around.

But I guess he's right. I listen to the instructions Felice is giving me.

"First, find a good tree. Next, put your toes in the bumps on the tree. Then, put your fingers on the higher bumps. After that pull yourself up and keep on doing it," he instructs.

"How do you pull yourself up without fingers?" I ask Felice.

"Easy. Just dig your fingers a little deeper from your costume."

I look at Titan. He's 10 yards away. Felice goes first. He does it, no problem.

I look at Titan. 5 yards.

I do as Felice said. When I'm halfway done, I feel something on my leg. It's pulling me downwards.

I look down and see Titan holding onto my leg. I squirm.

Then, I promise it was by accident, I accidentally kick Titan on the head. Felice laughs and I do too.

"He totally deserved that," says Felice, climbing down, because there's no use in hiding if the person, you're hiding from, is unconscious.

"We should carry him to the car and drive it to the police station, it's near the cheese shop," I say, pointing to Titan.

"And don't even think about driving the car, I am."

"Aww, man," Felice says.

Sorry, but I wouldn't let him drive a car with me inside it for all the money in the world.

I take Titan's legs and Felice takes his hands. I pull. Felice pushes. I pull again. Felice pushes again.

Finally, after 1000 minutes, more or less a lot hundred, we get Titan into the backseat and Felice joins me at the front.

I normally would never let him sit on the front seat, but for that matter I wouldn't let myself either.

Also, we're in another world so the rules are (I hope) different.

Hmm, I wonder how these things work. Well, the key's already in the lock so I don't have to worry about that.

Then I think you put your feet and push on the thingy at the bottom to go forward. And to stop, stop pushing. Easy enough.

But I hope we don't need to go backward. I have no idea how to do that. I buckle up and tell Felice to do the same.

"I don't know how to do that, Ara," Felice says.
Right, I forgot that he's still in a car seat and has no idea whatsoever how to do this.

I have a booster, so I know. I put the buckle on him the *right* way.

Then I push on the thingy and we rocket forward. We go past a red traffic light before I'm able to control the car.

"Wow! That was awesome!" Felice shouts.

"I can't believe that we passed a red light and you say 'Wow'," I mutter.

But it was a bit fun. Make that a lot fun. We get to the cheese shop in no time.

While we're at it we pass 6 red lights, nearly crash into 3 cars, hit the curb at least 20 times, almost trample a poor tree, drove over some flowers in a yard, and crushed a stop sign.

Needless to say, I am the worst at driving. For now. When I'm older I'll be the best at it. Titan's car is pretty damaged by now. But he won't be needing it when he's in jail.

We ask a lady pig where the police station is and we find it.

We go to the front desk and we see…

Bok and Luna, the police officer!!

He's saying what Titan has told him to do. We run over to him and he starts smiling.

"Do you have Titan?" Bok asks. I say "Yup!"

"Great!!" says a police officer. He has a badge that says 'Officer Scott'.

"I'll bring him here for a confession."

"Can I go too?" Felice asks me.

"Not without me," I say. We go with Officer Scott.

By now Titan is ok except for the huge bump on his head. Oopsies.

"You have a huge confession to make," the officer says. Titan hangs his head in defeat and he takes off his mask and costume.

Everyone gasps.

Chapter 9
The Truth

The shape of his head looks familiar. The shape of his ears looks familiar. The shape of his nose looks familiar. OMG.

Titan is a human in disguise.

"I'm human," Titan says, pointing out the obvious.

"Quick," I turn to Felice. "Go get Tom and Owen."

"Can't you go?" Felice says. I guess he doesn't want to miss the 'fun'.

"You," I say firmly, pointing to the door. Felice looks mad, but he doesn't argue. One of the upsides of being older. You get to boss your brother around. Felice storms out.

We're all silent for a bit.

I want an explanation from Owen and Tom. Could they be humans too? Are they evil? Are they all brothers? Are they all partners in crime? Were me and Felice just fooled? These questions swarm around my mind fogging it. In the meantime, Felice found Owen and Tom and I see them coming in. I jump up.

"I would like a full explanation!" I demand, angrily.

"Are you guys human like Titan? Are you really Titan's brothers or his partners in crime?"

"What?" Tom and Owen say together. Oh. I guess they're not partners or human. But that doesn't explain why they said that Titan was their brother.

"Um, my name is not Titan," says Titan.

"Really? Then what is it? Bob?" I huff. I will not believe anything from a villain.

"No, it's Edward," says Titan-who-says-his-name-is-Edward, rolling his eyes.

Edward? That name does not sound like someone who would try to kill two pigs and a wolf.

"I have proof too," says Titan-who's-not-really-Titan.

He gets out a wallet and shuffles through it. When he finds what he's looking for, he gives it to us.

It shows a person that looks like Titan and it says at the bottom: Edward Calvin. Oh! It's an ID card! It looks real enough to me.

"Ok, but you have to tell us the truth," I say.

Edward sighs and starts.

"A few months ago, in my country, people were trying to get some pigs to roast, so I came here and hunted some," he starts.

"Aha!" says police officer Luna.

"So, *you're* behind the disappearance of pigs."

"Yup," says Edward in a guilt.

"You're the person us wolves and pigs have been trying to catch for months?" Bok asks.

Edward nods. He continues.

"But soon the people in my town were getting bored of pigs and they said that they'd give anything for a wolf. It's harder to catch a wolf so I-"

"Wait," I say.

"Can't pigs just yell for help when they're captured?"

"No. The second they're out of their hometown, pigs start walking on four legs and stop talking," Edward explains.

"Now can I continue?"

We all nod yes.

"So, I tried to catch a wolf, but they were too fast. I decided to target one wolf, which is you," Edward says to Bok.

"I tricked you into thinking that I needed your help to eat two pigs because they were mean so that you would be fat enough, so that I could get a lot of money off you. To make sure that I planned everything correctly, I decided to ask Tom and Owen to let me live with them and they said yes. I would have gotten my way if it wasn't for you two," Edward says to us.

We have all been listening quietly, when I ask Tom and Owen "Why did you say that Edward was your brother?"

"Well, he's not really our brother, but our mom said he was close enough," they say, blushing.

"Well, you should tell your mom about Edward," says an officer with a badge that says: Officer Seith.

She turns to Edward. "You can come with us. I would like a more detailed explanation."

Officers Scott and Luna follow. That leaves me, Felice, Bok, Owen, and Tom.

"Um, you guys should go home," suggests Tom awkwardly.

"OK," I say.

"I should get going anyway. My parents will be worried sick," Bok says as he goes.

"So should we," I say, even though I have no idea what to do.

"Not without a celebration! We're going to invite all the pigs in Pown! Now, humans know not to hunt pigs, or else they'll meet the same end as Edward," Felice cheers. I look at my watch. Yikes! It's 6:00 A.M.

"Ok but we need to go in about one and a half hours," I tell them. That will give us half an hour to find the portal home.

"That's ok," Tom says.

One hour later the party is in full swing. We have turned the police station into a party place. I laugh and talk and giggle with some girl pigs, while Felice and some other pigs his age play some sort of game. While I am talking my watch falls off my hand. Whoops. But it's not broken.

My watch says 6:45. Ahhhhhhhh!

We have lost track of time. Oh no, oh no, oh no, oh no. "Felice," I hiss.

"Come on we need to go, we lost track of time." We quietly try to slip away, but Tom and Owen catch us.

"Where are you going?" They ask together.

"We really need to go. Remember when I said that we had to go after one and a half hours? Well, we forgot and now we only have half an hour to get back to our house."
"Hurry then!" says Tom.

"Goodbye!" Felice shouts, as we walk out the door.

The second we're out I start to feel dizzy. And then……………I'm falling into blackness.

Chapter 10
Home, sweet, home

The next thing I know, I'm back in the basement!

"You did very well, for your first mission," a voice says.

Huh? I look at the mirror. In it, I see a person with wings.

It's a fairy! Wait! Fairies are real?

"My name is Liliana," the fairy says.

"You did very well. Let me explain. When I send you on a mission, I will enchant different things from your house. When you finish the mission, say goodbye, and when you guys are alone, you will come back to where you were last in this house."

So that's how it works. But I have a question.

"How do we know the mission?" I ask, but already the fairy is fading away.

Me and Felice just stand there for a couple of seconds. Then I look at my watch. Ahhhhhhhhhhh!

It's 6:55. "Let's go," I whisper to Felice.

We race up the stairs quietly. When we're in the upstairs hallway, Felice goes to his room and I go to mine. Just as I slip into the cover, I hear thumps going down the stairs.

"Ara, Felice come down." My parents yell.

I go down for breakfast. After I'm dressed for school, I bring my book, The Three Little Pigs to read on the bus. Bus rides are so long.

When I open my book, I gasp. It's the new version of the book. As in, the way me and Felice changed the book.

We're in a book. Not only that, but also, we're one of the main characters.

When we get to school, I close the book and get off the bus.

✳ ✳ ✳ ✳ ✳ ✳ ✳ ✳ ✳ ✳ ✳ ✳ ✳ ✳ ✳ ✳

When I go to the library during recess to look at
the copy of The Three Little Pigs, it's exactly as before.

"Hi!" says another girl.

"Do you like to read?"

I nod.

"One of my favorite books is The Three Little Pigs, what's
yours?" She asks.

"I can't choose, but I like that one too," I say to her.

As we chat about our favorite books, I smile. I think, I have
a new best friend......

Epilogue

The next day, I go to the basement to see if there's anything new, and I see a letter on the floor. I open it up and read it.

Dear Ara and Felice,

So, that's the story of your first adventure, with many more to come.

Oh, anyways you are reading the words of me, Lilliana, the fairy stuck in the mirror. But I'm not really stuck in a mirror.

I am trapped in a story, but it will be very hard to get there. I am saving my magic for it, but in the meantime, I will send you into books which need your help.

Soon, I will tell you where I am trapped. I will give you 3 hints about where you will next go.

Hint 1. A princess cursed to death.
Hint 2. 100 years.
Hint 3. …Beauty.

Goodbye!

Your friend, Lilliana

About the author

Anushka is 8 years old and she is in grade 3. She wrote this book because magic books are the best, and the best magic books are when normal kids end up having adventures, so she decided to write one. Anushka enjoys reading, bike riding, and movies. She has a sister Arushi, in kindergarten.

Connect with Anushka On Social Media

SCAN HERE